C0-AMY-298
of
Missouri State Library
Jefferson City, MO
CMSU 181-84

92RH

McGRAW-HILL BOOK COMPANY

New York · St. Louis · Dallas · San Francisco

TO
DANIEL ARDIZZONE
AND
CRISTINA CAPPARUCCI

First distribution in the United
States of America by McGraw-Hill, Inc. 1968
First published in Great Britain by
Hamish Hamilton Ltd. 1967

Library of Congress Catalog Card Number: 68-12425

Printed in Great Britain

Long, long ago, in the city of Mulcaster, there lived a boy named Will. His father was a poor shoe-mender. He was a good boy and cheerful, but there was one thing wrong with him. He couldn't speak. Not a word did he say until he was almost seven. Then one day he opened his mouth and said:

"I see a man down yonder street
With pies and gingerbread to eat."

Everyone was delighted to hear little Will speak, for they had feared there was something wrong with him. They were all so surprised that no one noticed he had spoken in rhyme. That evening Will said:

"Now I have washed and fed,
I think I'll go to bed."

At this they were all astonished, and they were still more astonished when Will went on speaking verses. Everything he said was in rhyme. On a fine sunny morning he looked about him and said:

"It is a merry thing
To see the green grass spring
And high upon the wing
To hear the skylark sing."

But next day it was dull and stormy. Will looked out of the window and growled:

"I hate the stormy sky,
The black clouds overhead.
Roll by, black clouds, roll by,
Or we shall all be dead!"

I could tell you a hundred things Will said in that first week, and they were all in verse.

Now the people of Mulcaster did not like poetry. They called the little boy Rhyming Will, and made fun of him. Even his brothers and sisters laughed, and told him to speak properly, like other people.

But Will couldn't. However hard he tried, he just couldn't. He became very unhappy. How could he live in a place where people mocked him? So one day he said to himself:

"In Mulcaster I cannot stay:
I am resolved to run away."

He took some food and his little dog Spot, who never laughed at him, and set off on the road to London. About dinnertime a carrier gave him a lift. He handed Will a pie to eat, and another for Spot.

"Now don't try to thank me," said the carrier, "for I'm deaf as a post, and I can't hear a word you say."

When they came to London, the carrier put Will down at Charing

Cross. Spot barked their thanks, and wagged his tail vigorously.

Will went in search of lodgings. He found a friendly cobbler sitting outside his shop, and without a word took the hammer from the man's hand and finished the job. The cobbler could see that Will was a clever boy, so he offered to take him in and feed and clothe him in exchange for help in the shop. Will told the cobbler he could not help rhyming, and asked him not to laugh. He said:

"Pray do not laugh if every time
I talk to you, I speak in rhyme."

The cobbler didn't make fun of Will. They had all sorts of strange folk in London, he said, and Will was no stranger than others. In fact, Rhyming Will soon became a favorite in all the city, and people would stand and talk with him only to hear him talk poetry. Will was happy at last, and the cobbler was pleased because people brought their shoes to his shop only to hear Will speak in rhyme.

There was one thing the boy did not like – a large crowd. Too many people together made him nervous. Once, when a specially large number of people collected round him, he lifted his head from his work and began to speak.

"Oh what a c-crowd of p-people I see," he stammered.

Then he hesitated before going on.

"All standing round l-looking at me.
I w-wish they would all go back to their homes
And leave me –"

Again Will hesitated and then finished off:

– "And leave me alone."

Everyone laughed. Some rude fellows made fun of Will's bad rhyme. The boy turned red with confusion and ran indoors. Even Spot looked as if he was ashamed of his master and slunk away

with his tail between his legs. The cobbler, who had been standing near and had heard everything, was surprised. This had never happened before.

But the idle crowd melted away. Will came out and got on with his work. He was happy once more.

Soon it was Lord Mayor's day. There was to be a splendid reception. The new Lord Mayor was to entertain an important, rich Nabob from India. Now it was the custom in those days to give a feast to every important visitor; and the City Poet, whose name was Elkaner Settle, had to make up a poem and recite it to all the

company. But this year, on the very eve of the great day, Mr. Settle fell ill. He could not come to the banquet, and, what was worse, he had not made up a poem. The Lord Mayor was in a terrible state.

"What, no Ode?" he cried in despair. (In those days important poems were called 'Odes'.)

Then somebody told him about Will. At once the boy was sent for, and asked if he would recite an Ode at the feast. The Lord Mayor told him what to say, and Will promised to make it into a poem.

"Mind," said the Lord Mayor, "it must be a very special poem – an Ode, d'ye hear?"

Next day the Nabob was received with pomp and ceremony. He was given a magnificent banquet and various worthies made pompous speeches of welcome, which the Nabob listened to attentively.

At last it was Will's turn. He looked pale, but he smiled bravely as he was set high on a chair for the whole company to see and hear. The Lord Mayor told the company about Will's gift of rhyming, and

said he knew they were going to hear a truly fine Ode, every line rhyming smartly with the one next to it. Never, he said, had there been such a boy for rhymes. Mr. Settle himself couldn't do better.

Then a dreadful thing happened. Will opened his mouth, but nothing came out. The people nearest to him urged him to start. This made him more nervous than ever. How he wished that Spot was with him to give him courage. But of course dogs were not allowed at the Lord Mayor's feast. At last he made a mighty effort, and spoke out clearly for all to hear. This is what he said:

"My Lord Mayor, my Lord Nabob of India, your Worships, Ladies and Gentlemen, it gives me the very greatest pleasure to welcome our distinguished guest from over the sea to this our City of London. I hope you will be as happy here, Lord Nabob, as you are in India. May you enjoy health and wealth as long as you live!"

At this there was the most terrible confusion. People cried, "The Ode, the Ode!" But not another word could poor Will say. He blushed scarlet, jumped off his chair, and ran out of the hall.

The Ode
The Ode
The Ode
The Ode
The Ode

When he reached his lodgings, he told the cobbler what had happened, and how he had made a laughingstock of himself before all the fine ladies and gentlemen of London. It was a mercy, he said, that Queen Anne was kept indoors by a cold, or she would have been there.

"Whatever will happen to me?" asked Will. "Do you think I'll be shut in the Tower or have my head cut off?"

"Why, boy," said the cobbler, "you're talking like other folks now. You aren't talking in poetry like you used to."

It was true. From that time on, though Will could make up a poem if he chose, he could also talk in ordinary language, like you and me.

While Will was still wondering what would happen to him, a splendid carriage rolled up, and a dignified gentleman with a dark skin and a high turban asked to see the boy. To Will's amazement he saw that it was the Nabob from India. He was even more astonished when the Nabob handed him a purse with five gold coins. The Nabob told Will and the cobbler that he had been so pleased with

Will's speech of welcome that he had come in person to give him a special reward.

"You are a genius, my boy!" the Nabob said. "Everywhere I go, I have to listen to stuffy Odes in rhyme, as long as ten elephant trunks. I HATE ODES! If I had had to listen to one more poem after that banquet, I should have been ill. That was the best speech of welcome I have ever heard!"

"Hooray! Hooray!" shouted Will, and all the neighbors, who had come out of doors to see the fine coach, joined in the cheering. As for Spot, he wagged his tail and barked so loudly that he had to be given an extra juicy bone to keep him quiet.